Five reasons w love Mirabelle...

Mirabelle is magical and mischievous!

Mirabelle is half witch, half fairy, and totally naughty!

She loves making potions with her travelling potion kit!

Mirabelle loves sprinkling a sparkle of mischief wherever she goes!

She has a little baby dragon called Violet!

If you were going to start a business, what would you do?

The business I would like to start would be a teddy bear fashion house.
– Olivia, age 10

I'd make a place to teach children and adults to grow their own fruit and veg, and to care for the world.
– Caitlin, age 5

A glitter magic wand shop, to make people happy when they are sad.
– Thandie, age 7

I would like to set up a potion shop to sell mischievous spells.
– Vittoria, age 4

I would like to open a pet hotel to take care of the pets of witches, wizards, fairies, and vampires when they go on holiday.
– Elisa, age 7

We would like to own a shop with handmade flower crowns from our garden. The flower crowns have special glitter on them that give them magical powers.
– Sisters Julianna, age 7, Abigail, age 10

Family Tree

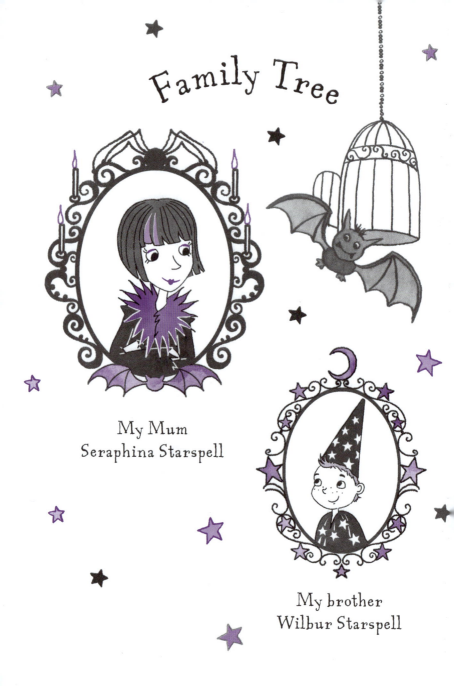

My Mum
Seraphina Starspell

My brother
Wilbur Starspell

My Dad
Alvin Starspell

Me!
Mirabelle Starspell

Violet

Illustrated by Mike Love, based on
original artwork by Harriet Muncaster

OXFORD
UNIVERSITY PRESS

Great Clarendon Street, Oxford OX2 6DP
Oxford University Press is a department of the University of Oxford.
It furthers the University's objective of excellence in research, scholarship,
and education by publishing worldwide. Oxford is a registered trade mark
of Oxford University Press in the UK and in certain other countries

Database right Oxford University Press (maker)

First published in 2023

British Library Cataloguing in Publication Data

Data available

ISBN: 978-0-19-278372-1

1 3 5 7 9 10 8 6 4 2

Printed in Great Britain by Bell and Bain Ltd, Glasgow

Paper used in the production of this book is a natural,
recyclable product made from wood grown in sustainable forests.
The manufacturing process conforms to the environmental
regulations of the country of origin.

MIX
Paper | Supporting
responsible forestry
FSC
www.fsc.org FSC® C007785

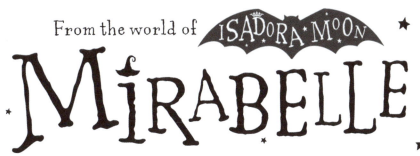

From the world of ISADORA MOON

MIRABELLE

Takes Charge

Harriet Muncaster

OXFORD
UNIVERSITY PRESS

Chapter ONE

It was a beautiful bright summer morning as I wheeled through the air towards Miss Spindlewick's Witch School for Girls. My hair flowed out behind me in the breeze, and the sun glinted off my pointed hat as I circled the playground, looking for my best friend, Carlotta. There she was! Gliding across the playground with two other witch girls, Kira and Tabitha.

Wait!

Gliding?

I flew closer, peered harder.

All three of them were wearing roller

skates! New, shiny, black and purple roller

skates. I knew exactly the ones because I had seen them advertised on TV before my brother Wilbur's favourite wizard game show.

The roller skates were sleek and sparkly.

Beautiful and *expensive*.

They had glittery silver stars all over them, and when you went really fast, sparks shot out from the heels. My eyes went big and round as I watched Carlotta whizz across the black tarmac. I couldn't help feeling a tiny bit jealous.

Well, maybe a *lot* jealous actually.

I landed my broom with a skid and hopped off it, my pet dragon Violet fluttering by my ear.

'MIRABELLE!' cried Carlotta, zooming towards me so fast that sparks shot out from her heels. She held out her arms, barrelling right into me so that we both tumbled over.

'Ouch!' I said, rubbing my elbow.

'Oops!' said Carlotta, rubbing her knee. 'I still haven't quite got the hang of these. Sorry, Mirabelle. Did I hurt you?'

'It's OK,' I said, begrudgingly. I couldn't take my eyes off her skates. They were *dazzling*. The silver stars glittered and twinkled like little fairy lights in the sunshine. Carlotta got unsteadily back onto her feet.

'Do you like them?' she asked. 'My uncle came to visit at the weekend. He bought them for me as a present!'

'I love them!' I replied wistfully.
'Can I have a go?'

'Oh, um . . . I guess so . . .' replied
Carlotta, not sounding very much like
she wanted me to have a go at all. Very
slowly, she bent down to undo the laces.

And then the bell rang. Witches all
around us in the playground began to
swarm into neat lines.

'Oh, never mind!' said Carlotta,
cheerfully. She hurriedly took the skates
off and put them in her bag so that our
strict teacher Miss Spindlewick wouldn't
see them. 'Maybe you can have a go at
the end of the day.'

But when the end of the day came,
Carlotta suddenly seemed very eager to
dash off.

'I promised I'd go to the park with
Kira and Tabitha,' she said. 'It's a good
place for skating. I'll see you tomorrow,
Mirabelle.'

Then she hopped onto her
broomstick and flew away.

I watched Carlotta disappear over the
tops of the trees with Kira and Tabitha.

Then I got onto my own broomstick and flew huffily up into the air. I knew why Carlotta hadn't invited me to go to the park with them. It was because she wanted her new roller skates all to herself. Well, of course she did! I would probably have felt the same way if *I* had new roller skates. But even so, I couldn't help feeling left out. Carlotta was supposed to be my best friend!

I flew despondently over the tops of the trees, towards the edge of the forest, where I saw Wilbur hovering in the air, waiting for me. Wilbur goes to a wizard school which is in a different direction to my witch school, but we always meet at the same spot to fly the rest of the way home together.

'You look glum,' said Wilbur when I had caught up to him. 'What's wrong?'

'Oh, it's *nothing*,' I said. 'Just that everyone seems to have a new pair of witch skates except me!'

'Oh, yeah,' said Wilbur. 'My friend George brought in a pair of those today. They look fun!'

'*So* much fun!' I sighed. 'I wish I had some!'

'They're just the same as normal roller skates though,' said Wilbur. 'Can't you magic some up with your fairy wand?'

Wilbur and I are both half fairy, although Wilbur doesn't like to admit it most of the time. Both of us have wands, though we hardly ever use them.

'It wouldn't be the same!' I complained. 'I'd never be able to conjure up a pair as good as the real *proper* ones! And I wouldn't know how to get them to spark either. No, I need Mum and Dad to buy me an *actual* pair right away!'

Wilbur raised his eyebrows.

'Good luck with that!' he said.

As soon as we arrived home, Wilbur disappeared off to the sitting room, and I heard him turn on the TV. The jingle jangle of the roller skate advert immediately floated out into the kitchen where I was busy rummaging in the cupboard for a chocolate biscuit. *I was being taunted by those roller skates from every angle!* I needed to get a pair for myself. As soon as possible!!

Stuffing a chocolate biscuit into my mouth, I hurried up the stairs to find Mum and Dad. They are usually around to greet us when Wilbur and I get home from school, but they've been so busy lately, developing a new product, that I think they lose track of time. Mum and Dad own their own beauty business concocting organic face creams, perfumes, and lipsticks. Mum uses her witchy potion magic to create the products and Dad oversees everything to make sure that it's all natural and good for the environment. Nature is very important to fairies!

I bounded all the way up the twirly staircase to the witch turret where I knew my parents would be.

'Mirabelle!' said Mum, looking up from her cauldron. She was wearing a pair of goggles and her cheeks were all smudged with black soot.

'Hello, my little witch-fairy,' said Dad as he busily leafed through some papers at a desk nearby. 'Did you have a good day at school?'

'Not really,' I said, truthfully. 'Everyone in the class has a new pair of witch skates. I really need a pair! Now! *Pleeeease?*'

'*Everyone?*' asked Mum.

'Well . . . Carlotta, Kira, and Tabitha,' I said, jutting out my chin. 'It *feels* like everyone! I can't join in with any of their games until I have some too.'

'I have a pair of old roller skates in the garage somewhere,' said Dad. 'From when I was about your age. They're pink with fairy wings on the back of them. I'll find them for you later.'

I stared at Dad in horror.

'Oh *no!*' I replied. 'There's a very specific pair that I want. They're black and sleek and shiny with stars all over them, and when you go really fast they send out sparks from the heels!'

'I think I've seen them advertised on the TV,' said Mum. 'They're very expensive, Mirabelle. Maybe you could have them for your birthday?'

'But my birthday's ages away!' I wailed.

Mum shrugged.

'If you can't wait that long, then you'll have to buy them yourself,' she said. 'You could earn some money by doing chores if you like. My cauldron needs a good clean!'

'And the garden needs weeding,' added Dad.

'Chores!' I said, dismayed.

'Mmm-hmm,' said Mum, going back to stirring her potion. 'Alvin, please could you pass me the jar of dried violet petals? I think the mixture needs more purple!'

I made my way back down the stairs to my bedroom, wondering if there was another, more *fun* way to make some money. Doing chores would be so boring! Maybe I could start a business just like Mum and Dad? They always seemed to be having fun together. But . . . I didn't really know enough about making beauty products. I needed to think of something else . . .

I wandered over to the window and put my chin on my hands, gazing outside into the garden. Over the fence, I could see next door's dogs running about—there was a big spotted dalmatian called Dotty and a small black yappy one called Dylis.

I liked Dotty and Dylis.
I always made sure to give
them a pat if we passed them
while out on the street. Our
neighbour Mrs Blue walked
them twice a day. I wondered
if Mrs Blue's feet ever got
tired. Maybe she could do
with some help? Some help in
return for *payment*.

I could start a dog-
walking business!

Why not?!

It would be much more
fun than doing chores!

I got changed as fast as

29

I could, rushed out of my bedroom and raced down the stairs, feeling excited. Dotty and Dylis could be my first customers! I would be such a good dog walker that Mrs Blue would be sure to tell all her friends. I would be making buckets of money in no time! The sleek, shiny witch skates would be *mine*!

Chapter TWO

'Tell Mum and Dad I've gone out for a bit,' I called to Wilbur, as I ran past the sitting room. 'I'm going to see if Mrs Blue needs any help walking her dogs. I'm starting a dog-walking business!'

'Uh, OK . . .' replied Wilbur through a mouthful of chocolate biscuits.

I left the house and ran down our

garden path, out of the gate, and then into Mrs Blue's front garden, which bloomed with summer flowers. There were puffy-looking marigolds that twinkled with permanent dewdrops, zingy zinnias boasting rainbow petals,

and powder-blue roses the colour of the sky.

Mrs Blue is also a witch. She loves her garden, and she can often be spotted outdoors, sprinkling spells onto her flowers.

I stood on the doorstep and smoothed down my clothes, noticing for the first time that there were stains on my dress. Oops! I hoped that Mrs Blue wouldn't notice. It was important to look *professional* for my first job! Hurriedly, I tried to hide the stains beneath my long hair. Then, I rang the doorbell, suddenly feeling a little bit nervous.

Tring a ling a ling!

'Mirabelle!' said Mrs Blue, opening the door. 'How lovely to see you!' She was wearing a pale lilac dress with a matching pointed hat and big horn-rimmed spectacles. Her hair was coiffed into soft pink curls. She smelled of lavender.

'Good afternoon, Mrs Blue,' I said politely. 'I've started a dog-walking business, and I was wondering if you'd like me to take Dotty and Dylis out?'

'Oh!' said Mrs Blue, sounding a little unsure. 'Well, my dear, they can be a bit of a handful. I don't know . . .'

'I'm *very* good with animals,' I said quickly. 'I'm absolutely certain I can handle them! I promise I'll keep them on their leads.'

I gave Mrs Blue my most beaming, reassuring smile.

How hard can dog walking be?

'We-eell,' said Mrs Blue again. 'I suppose if you keep them on their leads, it should be alright. Come inside and I'll show you what to do.'

I followed Mrs Blue into the house, wondering how complicated it could be!

'This is Dotty's lead,' said Mrs Blue, 'and this is Dylis's. You mustn't get them mixed up. Now, I'm going to give you a bag of dog treats. Dotty is allergic to these ones, so make sure to only give them to Dylis. Dylis is very particular about her treats, so don't get them mixed up with Dotty's!'

I nodded my head, eager to start the

walk, but it seemed Mrs Blue still had more to say.

'Now, Dotty has a tendency to pull on the lead,' she continued, 'so make sure that you hold it very tight!'

'Yes, Mrs Blue,' I replied.

'And,' she carried on, 'you need to watch out for rabbit holes. Dylis loves to . . .'

I started to zone out. It was hard to take in everything Mrs Blue was saying. I looked past her through the window and into the garden where the two dogs were now lying in the sun. I couldn't wait to clip on their leads and be in charge!

Eventually, after what felt like forever,

Mrs Blue called her dogs inside, and
Dotty and Dylis came bounding into the
house. When they saw me thcy jumped
up, pawing and licking. They were so
enthusiastic I almost fell over!

Mrs Blue helped me to put their leads on, and then finally I was off! Walking down the garden path, out onto the street, and down a little footpath that led to a big field behind the houses. Well, actually I was *running* not walking because Mrs Blue had been right about Dotty. She loved to pull on the lead. And she was strong!! I was

starting to get quite puffed out as I was
dragged along behind her.

'Slow, Dotty!' I called. 'Slow!'

But Dotty didn't slow down. When
we got to the big field she started to pull
harder, panting and straining and leaping
this way and that. Her lead was getting
all tangled up with Dylis's! My arm was
beginning to ache.

'Slow, Dotty!' I said, more forcefully
this time. 'Do you want a treat? You can
have a treat if you stop pulling!'

At the word 'treat' both dogs
immediately turned to look at me, sitting
down on the grass.

'Good girls,' I said, feeling relieved. I got the two bags of treats out of my pockets and looked at them. Which ones were Dotty's and which ones were Dylis's? Mrs Blue had told me, but now I couldn't remember!

'Um . . .' I said, staring at the two bags in confusion.

The dogs were getting impatient. Dotty stood up and bounced towards me, sniffing at the bags.

'Oh dear,' I said. 'I can't remember which ones are yours! And what if I get it wrong? I can't give you treats that you might be allergic to. That wouldn't be good for business. I had better not give you any at all!'

I stuffed the bags of treats back into my pocket, feeling flustered. Dotty and Dylis both began to bark at me crossly.

'I'm sorry!' I said, shrugging helplessly.

Dylis began to run round and round in circles, her shrill yappy bark hurting

my ears, and Dotty turned away in a huff, beginning to pull on the lead again. This time my grip wasn't so tight. I had been distracted by the whole treat fiasco! The lead slipped from my fingers, unwound itself before I could stop it, and then Dotty bounded away across the field, barking happily.

'Oh no!' I said as I watched her disappear through a hedge. *'Oh no!'*

I held on tightly to Dylis's lead as I began to run across the field towards the hedge where Dotty had disappeared. This was going to be bad for business! I should have listened more carefully to Mrs Blue's instructions!

'DOTTY!' I yelled. 'DOTTY! COME BACK!'

I wiped my forehead with my hand. Dog walking was turning out to be far more stressful than I had imagined. I couldn't believe that I had lost Dotty! Mrs Blue would be distraught if one of her beloved pets went missing!

'DOTTTTYYYY!' I yelled again.

'Woah!' came a voice from behind me, and I whirled round to see Wilbur standing there. I had never felt so relieved to see my big annoying brother.

'Mum sent me to tell you that it's dinner time,' he said.

'Oh,' I replied. 'Well, I can't come

to dinner right now. I have to find Dotty!
She's run off! Can you help me find her,
Wilbur? Please?'

Wilbur smirked.

'I thought you were starting a
business for dog *walking*, not dog *losing*!'
he said.

I stamped my foot on the ground. I
didn't have time for Wilbur's teasing.

'Just help me, will you?' I said. 'It's an
emergency!'

'Oh fine!' replied Wilbur and he rolled
up his sleeves pompously. 'I'll do a bit of
wizard magic. A retrieving spell! That
should bring Dotty back. We learned how
to do retrieving spells last week at school.'

I stared at Wilbur, feeling a little bit unsure. Sometimes Wilbur's spells didn't *always* go to plan.

'I was thinking more of looking for her with our eyes,' I said.

But Wilbur had already started. He put his hands out in front of him and wiggled his fingers. Then he said a load of words that sounded like gobbledygook to me and let out a *hooooowl*! I had to bite my lip to try not to laugh.

'There!' said Wilbur, opening his eyes again,

and to my amazement, Dotty emerged
from one of the bushes and came bounding
towards us. I immediately clipped her onto
the lead.

'Thank you, Wilbur!' I said.

Together we took the dogs back to
Mrs Blue.

'They look like they've had a lovely time!' she said. 'Same time tomorrow, Mirabelle?'

'Oh . . . er . . . I'm not sure,' I said. 'I think I might be closed for business actually.'

'What a shame!' said Mrs Blue. 'Well, never mind!'

She handed me some coins, and I took them gratefully before turning and hurrying as fast as I could back to my own house with Wilbur trailing behind.

A dog-walking business was not for me!

That evening at dinner, I laid the coins out on the table and counted them. There

definitely weren't enough to buy the
beautiful shiny witch skates, but it was a
start at least!

'I need to think of a new business
idea,' I said to Mum and Dad.

'Or you could just do a few chores?'
suggested Mum.

'The tomatoes need picking in the greenhouse,' said Dad.

'No!' I replied. 'I want to start a business!'

'OK,' Mum said, shrugging. 'Well, good luck! It's a lot of work having your own business.'

'There are costs,' added Dad. 'Employees to pay.'

That reminded me. I scooped up half of the coins on the table and handed them to Wilbur. I knew it was the right thing to do. If it hadn't been for Wilbur then Dotty might have been lost forever.

'Uh, thanks, Mirabelle,' said Wilbur. 'But I'm not your *employee*.'

'I know,' I said. 'But I was grateful for your help today.'

Wilbur didn't say anything but his cheeks went a bit pink, and he looked pleased.

Chapter THREE

That night as I lay in bed, my mind went round and round. What sort of business could I start? It needed to be something fun and interesting. I fell asleep thinking of ideas, and I was still thinking of ideas when I arrived at school the next morning, landing on the playground with a skid. I was early for once, but Carlotta was already there.

'Mirabelle!' she cried breathlessly, running up to me and holding out her new pair of roller skates. 'I'm sorry I didn't let you have a go with these yesterday. I feel really bad about not inviting you to the park. Here! Have a go with them now!'

She thrust the skates into my arms, looking guilty. I noticed that today she was wearing a new bracelet with lots of pretty charms hanging from it.

I looked around to check that Miss Spindlewick wasn't anywhere nearby. Then I whipped off my shoes and put the skates on. They felt wobbly at first, but with the help of Carlotta keeping me steady, I was soon gliding around the playground. Finally, she let go of my hand and I went whizzing across the tarmac, sparks shooting out of my heels. It felt amazing! It was better than flying!

'I love them!' I cried. 'I want a pair of my own so badly!'

The playground was getting busier
now. I knew the bell was about to ring at
any moment. And then Miss Spindlewick
would come outside. I sat down on the
ground to take the skates off.

'Listen, Carlotta,' I said. 'I *have* to

have a pair of my own! Even more so now
that I've tried yours! I've had an idea. I'm
going to start my own business. I'm going
to earn some money to buy my own pair
of witch skates.'

'That's a great idea!' said Carlotta.

'What are you going to do?'

'Well, that's the problem,' I replied.
'I can't think of anything!'

'Hmm,' said Carlotta.

As we thought hard, my eyes suddenly fell on the bracelet around Carlotta's wrist. The little silver charms hanging from it were very pretty. There was a tiny broomstick, a miniature cauldron, a black cat with green crystal eyes, a sprinkling of stars . . .

'I could sell bracelets!' I said. 'Like yours!'

Carlotta held her wrist out, and we both inspected the bracelet carefully.

'I could easily make them,' I said

confidently. 'You can help me! It will be fun!'

'OK!' replied Carlotta. 'But first, we should ask around and check that witches will want to buy them. There's no point making loads if we can't sell them.'

'Market research,' I said knowingly.

Mum and Dad were always going on about market research.

As soon as we got into the classroom, I took Carlotta by the wrist and began to drag her around the room.

'What do you think?' I asked the other witches. 'Would you buy one of these?'

There were lots of nods and gasps of admiration. Everyone seemed to think Carlotta's bracelet was very pretty. Carlotta looked pleased to be getting so many compliments. Then Miss Spindlewick came into the room, and I hurriedly scooted over to my desk.

'I think we'll definitely have customers!' I whispered to Carlotta.

That afternoon I went to the craft shop in the town and spent the money that I had earned from dog walking. I bought beads and string, paint, glue, glitter, and clay so that I would be able to fashion tiny charms like the ones on Carlotta's bracelet.

'What's all that for?' asked Wilbur, who had been waiting for me outside the shop.

'My jewellery-making business!' I told him excitedly.

That night, I stayed up late making bracelets.

'You need to go to sleep, Mirabelle!' said Mum when she came to kiss me goodnight and found me sitting up in bed, threading beads onto a piece of string. 'And don't get glue on your duvet!'

'I'll go to sleep soon,' I promised her.

But before long, the summer sky

outside my window grew dark, and the stars began to twinkle. Still, I sat up in bed, rolling clay between my hands and shaping it into little charms—miniature pointed hats, tiny potion bottles, cauldrons, little black cats, and purple dragons.

I worked as fast as I could, slopping paint onto them and showering glitter everywhere. They weren't looking quite as neat as I had hoped, but it didn't matter. Because I was starting to have another idea . . .

A brilliant idea, that would make my bracelets even better than Carlotta's.

I could sell *enchanted* charms!

Everyone would want to buy them!

It was almost midnight, but I still had time to make the potion if I worked fast.

I hopped out of bed and tiptoed over to my bookcase, pulling out a spellbook and flicking through it to find a potion that would work.

There!

Enchant clothes and accessories
to make the wearer:

Sparkle,

Smell delicious,

Attract singing birds.

I reached for my small, travel-sized
cauldron and my collection of potion
ingredients, trying very hard to not make
any clinking sounds with the bottles. I
didn't want to wake Mum and Dad! They
wouldn't be pleased if they knew I was
still awake.

Beneath the glow of my fairy wand,
I began to make the first potion—the one

that would make the wearer sparkle. I poured in the main ingredients and then added a dash of stardust. The mixture twinkled in my cauldron as I stirred it three times, muttering the words to the spell. When it was ready and bubbling, I grabbed a handful of the charms and dropped them into the cauldron, making sure that they got coated in the magic.

Next, I added some vanilla-scented perfume to the mixture and dropped in some more charms. Those ones should make the wearer smell really nice! Finally, I added five soft white feathers and stirred in the last of the charms.

It was done!

I laid all the charms out to dry and then fell into bed, exhausted.

'Mirabelle!' came Mum's voice through my dreams the next morning. 'Wake up! You'll be late for school.'

I opened my eyes blearily and sat up in bed.

'Why have you got beads stuck to your cheek?' asked Mum, frowning. 'What time did you go to sleep last night?'

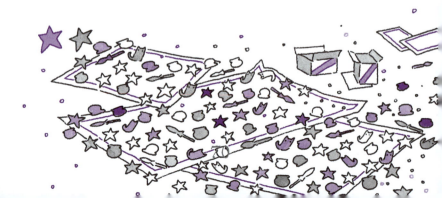

Then she looked around my room
and noticed the empty cauldron and all the
charms laid out next to it. She narrowed
her eyes and they went all dark and
dangerous like two glinty blackcurrants.
I held my breath. My mum can be a bit
scary when she's cross.

'I don't think I even *want* to know
what you've been up to, Mirabelle
Starspell!' she said, and I let out a sigh of
relief. 'Just stop right now with whatever
it is you're doing and we'll say no more
about it. Get downstairs for breakfast,
please!'

And then she swept out of the room.

I jumped out of bed and scooped up

all the charms, hurriedly threading them
onto the bracelets as fast as I could.

'MIRABELLE!' shouted Mum from downstairs.

I pulled my clothes on so fast that I got my dress on back to front. Then I stuffed all the finished charm bracelets into a bag and ran down the stairs with my unbrushed hair flying out behind me.

Mum looked at me suspiciously as I spooned fairy flakes into my mouth as fast as I could.

'Come on, Mirabelle!' said Wilbur. 'We'll be late!'

'I'm *coming*!' I replied.

Chapter FOUR

When I got to school Miss Spindlewick was already in the playground and witches were already beginning to line up. I landed on the black tarmac with a skid and hurried to my class line, nudging in behind Carlotta.

'Did you make the bracelets?' she whispered.

'Yes!' I said. 'I'll show them to you later. There isn't time to try and sell them now. We'll have to wait until morning break!'

All through the first lesson, I tapped my foot impatiently on the floor beneath my desk. I couldn't concentrate on *anything*! Miss Spindlewick kept glaring at me.

'If I had wanted such an annoying soundtrack to our lesson this morning,' she said, 'I would have brought a woodpecker into class.'

Everyone tittered.

Finally, *finally*, it was break time. I was first out of the classroom, running down the echoey hallways and out onto the playground.

'Carlotta!' I said breathlessly. 'We need to set up a stall! Quick! Go and get a table from inside!'

'I can't just go and *get* a table!' said Carlotta. 'Why don't you just lay all the bracelets out on the bench? It will be like a stall.'

'OK,' I said and opened my backpack, taking out handfuls of bracelets and starting to lay them out on the bench.

'What do you think?' I asked.

'They look . . . good,' said Carlotta. But she sounded slightly unsure. 'I mean, some of them *are* a *tiny* bit messy. But I'm sure no one will notice.'

'I think we need a sign,' I said.
'Carlotta, make a sign!'

'Um, OK,' replied Carlotta, scrabbling
in her bag for pen and paper.

Witches were beginning to crowd
around us now, interested in what was
going on.

'It's a shop!' I told everyone proudly. 'You can buy my bracelets. They have enchanted charms on them!'

'Ooh!' said Tabitha, picking up a particularly sparkly bracelet. One of the charms immediately dropped off.

'That one's faulty,' I said quickly, snatching the bracelet from her and thrusting a different one into her hands instead.

Tabitha looked at the new bracelet I had given her.

'What are the charms meant to be?' she asked.

'Can't you *tell*?' I replied, starting to feel frustrated. '*That* one is a black cat! *That* one is a cauldron, and *that* one is a tiny purple dragon. Do you want to buy it?'

Tabitha put the bracelet back down on the bench.

'I'll think about it,' she said and then walked away. I turned to Carlotta, and

Carlotta looked at me and shrugged. Other witches started to pick up the bracelets and inspect them. Glitter and charms began to fall off all over the place.

'Did you make them in a bit of a rush?' whispered Carlotta.

'No!' I said crossly. 'I just made them *quickly*!'

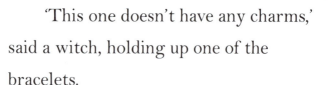

'This one doesn't have any charms,' said a witch, holding up one of the bracelets.

'Oh, give it to me,' said Carlotta, smiling politely. 'I can fix it for you!'

'No!' I said, starting to feel hot. '*I'll* fix it! They're my bracelets! You finish writing the sign, Carlotta.'

Carlotta frowned.

'But I have an idea how to make the bracelets better,' she said. 'I can help you, Mirabelle!'

'I don't want that kind of help!' I said a bit too snappily. 'Your job is just to help with the stall.'

Carlotta stared at me.

'You're being very bossy, Mirabelle!' she said.

'No, I'm not!' I said. 'I'm just trying to run a business. And you promised to be my employee!'

'I never promised to be your employee. I just said I'd help!' said Carlotta, sticking out her chin. 'And if I *was* your employee, you'd be a horrible boss! You haven't said please once! I'm resigning.'

'Well . . . fine then!' I spluttered. 'You won't get any of my profit!'

'I don't want any of your profit!' said Carlotta, and she stomped away to find Tabitha and Kira.

83

Huffily, I turned back to my stall. I didn't have time to think about Carlotta right now. I had a product to sell!

'What do the enchantments do?' asked Lavinia, holding up one of the bracelets and waving it in the air.

'Lots of things,' I replied, feeling flustered. 'Do you want to buy one and find out?'

Lavinia shrugged.

'Um . . . I guess so,' she said reluctantly. She dug in her skirt pocket for some coins and sprinkled them into my hand. Then she slipped the bracelet on. Suddenly, her skin became all twinkly, and two birds appeared above her head,

chirping away.
A delicious vanilla
scent filled the air.

'Ooh!' said witches
all around. But they
stepped a few paces
back from the flapping
birds. Hurriedly, Lavinia
took the bracelet off and
stuffed it into her pocket.
Immediately, the birds, sparkles,
and vanilla scent disappeared.

'I like the *sparkles*,' she said. 'But
I think I'll wear it later. Bye, Mirabelle!'

Witches began to drift away from
my stall.

'Bracelets for sale!' I called. 'Bracelets for sale!'

By the end of break time, I was standing all alone by the bench.

I had sold one bracelet.

One!

Despondently, I began to pack all my wares away. Why didn't witches want to buy my bracelets? I know they looked a *little* bit messy, and some of them were a bit broken, but I still thought they looked nice. And they had the enchantments too! The cheeping birds might get a bit annoying after a while, but I had thought the witches would like them as a novelty.

Back in the classroom, Carlotta sat with her back to me, and at lunchtime, she went and sat with Kira and Tabitha. By the end of the day, I felt really lonely and cross.

'I'll show Carlotta!' I thought as I kicked off from the ground on my broomstick. 'I don't need her help. I'll sell all my bracelets tomorrow!'

I just needed to work out how . . .

That afternoon, as I flew home with Wilbur, I had an idea.

What about using a potion on the charm bracelets?

A persuasion potion!

I knew there was a ready-made one on the kitchen counter in a squeezy bottle. Mum and Dad use it on our food sometimes to make it easier for Wilbur and me to eat our vegetables. What would happen if I used it on the charm bracelets?

As soon as I got home, I grabbed the bottle of persuasion potion and ran upstairs to my bedroom with it. Then I tipped all the charm bracelets into my cauldron and squeezed the whole bottle of shimmery, gloopy potion onto them. I made sure they were all completely covered, and then I took the bracelets out one by one, laying them out to dry.

'Mirabelle?' came Mum's voice, from the potion room. 'Mirabelle, are you home from school?'

I jumped up, fast as lightning.

'I'm coming!' I called, racing out of the room and slamming the door behind me. The last thing I needed was Mum coming to see what I was up to.

That evening, I packed all the charm bracelets into my schoolbag before Mum came in to say goodnight.

'It's nice and tidy in your bedroom,' she remarked. 'And you're in bed nice and early. Are you feeling OK, Mirabelle?'

'I just want to have a good sleep,' I said as I kissed her goodnight. 'I have a busy day tomorrow.'

Chapter FIVE

The following morning I woke up on time and leapt out of bed.

Today was the day!

I was going to sell LOADS of charm bracelets, I was sure of it!

And then the sleek and shiny witch skates would be mine!

I made sure to brush my hair until it

shined and put my dress on the right way round. Then I left for school feeling smug.

Because I had been so organized, I was one of the first witches to arrive at the playground. Miss Spindlewick was nowhere to be seen, so I quickly set up my stall of bracelets on the bench again.

They looked lovely, all glittering and twinkling in the sunshine.

Soon witches started to arrive. I saw Carlotta touch down on the tarmac, but she ignored me and walked off in another direction.

'Ooh!' said Tabitha coming over to look at the bracelets. 'I love the look of these, Mirabelle! Can I buy one? I've got lunch money I can give you!'

'Of course!' I grinned, holding out my hand for the money.

Tabitha took a bracelet and slipped it on. Immediately, that lovely vanilla scent filled the air, and three birds came fluttering over, cheeping and chirping.

'I want what she's got!' said a witch nearby and hurried over to take a look at my bracelets.

'That one, please!' she said, beginning to rummage in her schoolbag. 'I know I have some money somewhere. I was going to use it to pay my library fine!'

Witches were swarming over to my stall now, all jostling and nudging to get a look at the bracelets.

'Slow down!' I gasped as I tried to keep up with the shower of coins that were thrown towards me. One by one, the bracelets quickly disappeared until there were none left.

'I'll make more,' I promised the disappointed little group of witches who had been at the back of the queue. 'I'll bring them tomorrow!'

I heard the bell ring and hurriedly brushed the glitter off the bench. Then I walked away nonchalantly before Miss Spindlewick came out and saw me. I felt elated! My pockets were so heavy with coins that I knew I had earned enough money to buy three pairs of witch skates! Everyone had *loved* my bracelets! I decided to ignore the fact that I had put a persuasion potion on them. Surely it couldn't have been *that* strong? I felt sure that all my customers had only given me their money because they really wanted to.

But now that I wasn't focusing on the rush of witches all clamouring for my bracelets, I started to notice that it was very noisy in the playground. There were hundreds of birds fluttering and flapping, cheeping and chirping over everyone's heads. Feathers were falling like rain! I must have put too much of the potion on some of the charms because some of the birds weren't cheeping nicely—they were screeching and squawking! I was starting to get a little bit of a headache too, from the extremely strong scent of vanilla that seemed to be *everywhere.* It was so strong it was hurting the inside of my nose! And lastly, every witch who had bought a bracelet was twinkling. But some of them were fizzing and sparking like fireworks!

Uh-oh!

For the first time that morning, I started to feel a little worried. *What would Miss Spindlewick think?*

Witches all over the playground were getting into their lines now. I hurried over to mine, feeling a knot of dread inside my stomach.

'Take the bracelet off!' I whispered to the witch in front of me—Kira. She seemed to be sparking particularly brightly.

'Why?' asked Kira, with a glazed
expression on her face.

'Just do it!' I hissed, starting to feel
panicked.

But Kira just smiled and turned around
to face the great front doors.

'Cheep, cheep! Squawk, squawk!' went the
birds fluttering above all our heads.

I watched anxiously as the great
front doors of the school opened and Miss
Spindlewick came out into the playground.

She looked around.

She frowned.

She narrowed her eyes.

'*What* has been going on here?' she
asked.

'We've all bought bracelets from
Mirabelle!' piped up one of the witches.
'Aren't they brilliant?!'

She held up her wrist, waving it in
the air. Miss Spindlewick raked her fierce
dark glinty eyes across all the witches
in the playground until she found me.
I cowered in my line.

'All of you! Take the bracelets off!'
she ordered. 'I can't bear this infernal
cheeping!'

Witches all around looked confused.

'But they're so pretty!' said Lavinia,
her eyes dancing with reflected sparkles.

'We *can't* take them off!' said someone
else.

Miss Spindlewick pursed her lips, and two spots of angry pink colour appeared on her cheeks. I felt my knees begin to tremble.

'You will all stay out here in the playground then,' she said. 'Until further notice. *Mirabelle Starspell*, follow me!'

I forced my legs to move towards the great front doors of the school. And then I forced them to walk down the echoey hallways, following Miss Spindlewick to the classroom.

'MIRABELLE STARSPELL!' she said with her hands on her hips. '*What* is the meaning of this?!'

I swallowed hard, feeling tears begin to prick at the back of my eyes.

'I'm sorry, Miss Spindlewick,' I gabbled. 'I just wanted to earn some money to buy a pair of witch skates.

The same ones that Carlotta and Kira and Tabitha have. I thought I'd start a business selling enchanted charm bracelets, but it's all gone a bit wrong!'

'*Very* wrong, I should say!' said Miss Spindlewick.

I bowed my head.

'I put a potion on the bracelets so witches would buy them,' I whispered.

Miss Spindlewick didn't say anything for a moment, and I didn't dare look up.

'I just wanted to sell more bracelets,' I said in a small voice. 'But now I think it was the wrong thing to do.'

'It was *definitely* the wrong thing,' said Miss Spindlewick firmly. 'You must never use potions to make people do things they don't want to do.'

I nodded, feeling the weight of the money in my pockets and suddenly wishing that it wasn't there at all. It felt like bad money. Like I hadn't earned it fair and square.

'You will remove the potion from the bracelets and give a refund to *every* single witch who bought one,' said Miss Spindlewick. 'I'll mix up a counter-potion for you to use. And then, as punishment, you will stay in at lunchtime and clean the cauldrons for a whole week!'

'A week?!' I said, dismayed.

'It will be *two* weeks if you argue back!' snapped Miss Spindlewick.

I didn't dare say anything else.

After Miss Spindlewick had mixed up the counter-potion, I took it outside and went around the whole playground, sprinkling little drops of it onto the bracelets.

'Why did I buy this?' asked Kira, confused.

'Um, I put a potion on it,' I mumbled, embarrassed. 'But here, you can have the money back.'

I thrust a handful of coins towards her.

'You may as well keep the bracelet too,' I said.

'Oh,' said Kira. 'Well, it's OK, I don't really want it,' and she handed the bracelet back to me. I felt a bit hurt. The same happened with a lot of the other witches, but a few of them decided they wanted to keep them.

'They *are* very glittery!' said Tabitha. 'And I like being sparkly! I think I'll take the bird charm off though. It's a bit annoying.'

Soon I had a schoolbag full of bracelets and pockets empty of money. Even though I now knew I couldn't buy the witch skates, I felt lighter. My head felt clearer. I looked for Carlotta and saw her glancing at me from across the playground. I felt a pang of guilt. I had got so swept away with running my business that I hadn't thought about anything other than money!

I hurried over to my best friend. 'Carlotta,' I said breathlessly. 'I'm

really sorry I was a horrible boss! Can we be friends again? I miss you.'

Carlotta smiled.

'I miss you too,' she said. 'Even though you *were* a very bossy boss. I can't believe you put potions on the bracelets to get witches to buy them!'

'I know,' I said, hanging my head. 'I got carried away with it all.'

'Listen,' said Carlotta. 'I have an idea for how to make the bracelets better. Let's work as partners. We can *both* be the boss! And we can work together to make the bracelets really good.'

'Oh . . . I don't know,' I replied. 'I'm not sure I want to be in the bracelet business any more. It's quite stressful. I thought running a business would be easy, but now I realize how much hard work my mum and dad must put into theirs. I think I might just do some chores to earn some money instead.'

Carlotta shrugged.

'OK,' she said, looking a little disappointed.

'How about we just make them for fun instead though?' I suggested. 'For ourselves! Do you want to come round to my house after school today? We can make bracelets together! I've still got loads of beads and clay left. You can show me how to make them better!'

Carlotta brightened.

'That sounds perfect,' she replied.

Chapter SIX

Carlotta and I were sitting in the kitchen after school that afternoon, eating chocolate biscuits and making bracelets together when Mum and Dad came bursting into the room. They both looked worn out but very happy.

'We've done it!' crowed Mum. 'We've found the magic formula for the new black and purple striped lipsticks we've been trying to make!'

'Ooh!' said Carlotta. 'Stripy lipstick?'

'Yes!' Dad beamed and produced a little tube from behind his back. 'It's called the *Mirabelle* range!'

I felt a warm feeling sparkle inside me.

'Do you want to try it?' asked Dad.

I took the lipstick and painted it onto my lips while looking into a little hand mirror that Mum held up. Then I handed it to Carlotta.

'Stripy lips!' we both said, staring at each other with glee.

We looked wonderfully witchy!

'Phew, it works!' said Dad. 'Time for a celebration, I think. Let's go out for dinner when Wilbur gets home from his after-school club. Carlotta can come too!'

Carlotta and I beamed happily at each other.

'Oh, and that reminds me,' said Dad. 'I dug out my old fairy roller skates for you, Mirabelle. They're on the porch.'

'Roller skates!' said Carlotta. 'That means we can skate together!'

'Oh . . . erm. . . yes,' I replied. 'But they're not proper witch skates like yours they're—'

'Who cares?!' said Carlotta. 'They *work*, don't they?'

'I guess so,' I replied.

'Let's go and skate then!' said Carlotta, jumping down from her chair and tugging at me.

I picked up Dad's roller skates from the porch, and together we made our way out into the garden. Carlotta put on her witch skates and I put on my dad's old fairy skates. We began to whizz up and down the garden path, going faster and faster, whooshing and spinning. It felt amazing. It felt like flying! And I realized it didn't really matter that my roller skates weren't the sleek and shiny expensive ones or that they didn't have sparks coming out from the heels. They worked! I could go just as fast as Carlotta in them!

Suddenly I felt a little bit bad that I had been so ungrateful. It was very kind of Dad to give me his old skates. *Maybe* I

wasn't even so bothered about having a pair of sleek and shiny black witch skates after all. I could just keep using the fairy skates.

And *that* would mean I wouldn't have to do any extra chores!

Harriet Muncaster

Harriet Muncaster, that's me! I'm the author and illustrator of two young fiction series, Mirabelle and Isadora Moon. I love anything teeny tiny, anything starry, and everything glittery.

From the world of ISADORA MOON

MIRABELLE
Gets up to Mischief

Half witch, half fairy, totally naughty!

Harriet Muncaster

From the world of ISADORA MOON

MIRABELLE
Has a Bad Day

Half witch, half fairy, totally naughty!

Harriet Muncaster

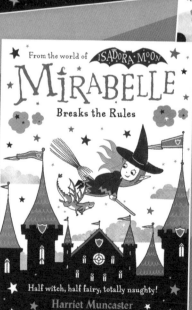

From the world of ISADORA MOON

MIRABELLE
Breaks the Rules

Half witch, half fairy, totally naughty!

Harriet Muncaster

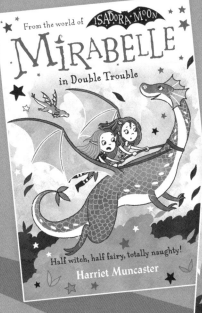

From the world of ISADORA·MOON

MIRABELLE
in Double Trouble

Half witch, half fairy, totally naughty!
Harriet Muncaster

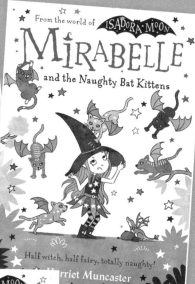

From the world of ISADORA·MOON

MIRABELLE
and the Naughty Bat Kittens

Half witch, half fairy, totally naughty!
Harriet Muncaster

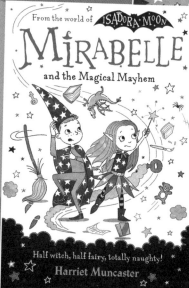

From the world of ISADORA·MOON

MIRABELLE
and the Magical Mayhem

Half witch, half fairy, totally naughty!
Harriet Muncaster

ISADORA MOON
Goes to School
Half vampire, half fairy, totally unique!
Harriet Muncaster

ISADORA MOON
Goes Camping
Half vampire, half fairy, totally unique!
Harriet Muncaster

ISADORA MOON
Has a Birthday
Half vampire, half fairy, totally unique!
Harriet Muncaster

ISADORA MOON
Goes to the Ballet
Half vampire, half fairy, totally unique!
Harriet Muncaster

ISADORA MOON
Gets in Trouble
Half vampire, half fairy, totally unique!
Harriet Muncaster

ISADORA MOON
Goes on a School Trip
Half vampire, half fairy, totally unique!
Harriet Muncaster

ISADORA MOON
Goes to the Fair
Half vampire, half fairy, totally unique!
Harriet Muncaster

ISADORA MOON
Makes Winter Magic
Half vampire, half fairy, totally unique!
Harriet Muncaster

ISADORA MOON
Has a Sleepover
Half vampire, half fairy, totally unique!
Harriet Muncaster

ISADORA MOON
Puts on a Show
Half vampire, half fairy, totally unique!
Harriet Muncaster

ISADORA MOON
Goes on Holiday
Half vampire, half fairy, totally unique!
Harriet Muncaster

ISADORA MOON
Goes to a Wedding
Half vampire, half fairy, totally unique!
Harriet Muncaster

ISADORA MOON
Meets the Tooth Fairy
Half vampire, half fairy, totally unique!
Harriet Muncaster

ISADORA MOON
and the Shooting Star
Half vampire, half fairy, totally unique!
Harriet Muncaster

ISADORA MOON
Gets the Magic Pox
Half vampire, half fairy, totally unique!
Harriet Muncaster

ISADORA MOON
Under the Sea
Half vampire, half fairy, totally unique!
Harriet Muncaster

Get ready to
meet Isadora's
mermaid friend,
Emerald!